W9-BSF-065

My Chincoteague Pony

Susan Jeffers

HYPERION BOOKS FOR CHILDREN
NEW YORK

To Peter and Madeline Myers, Brandon and Amelia Cook,
Rachel Resto, James Myers, and Julia Jeffers

Special thanks to Karen Murphy, the proprietor of the Chincoteague Roxy Theater,
and *Eastern Shore Times* reporter Jennifer Cording

Copyright © 2008 by Susan Jeffers

All rights reserved. Published by Hyperion Books for Children, an imprint of Disney
Book Group. No part of this book may be reproduced or transmitted in any form or by
any means, electronic or mechanical, including photocopying, recording, or by any information storage and retrieval system, without written permission from the publisher.

For information address

Hyperion Books for Children, 114 Fifth Avenue, New York, New York 10011-5690.

First Edition   5 7 9 10 8 6 4   Printed in Singapore

F850-6835-5-09335

Reinforced binding

Library of Congress Cataloging-in-Publication Data on file

This book is set in 20-pt. Pabst.

ISBN-13: 978-1-4231-0023-2

ISBN-10: 1-4231-0023-9

Visit www.hyperionbooksforchildren.com

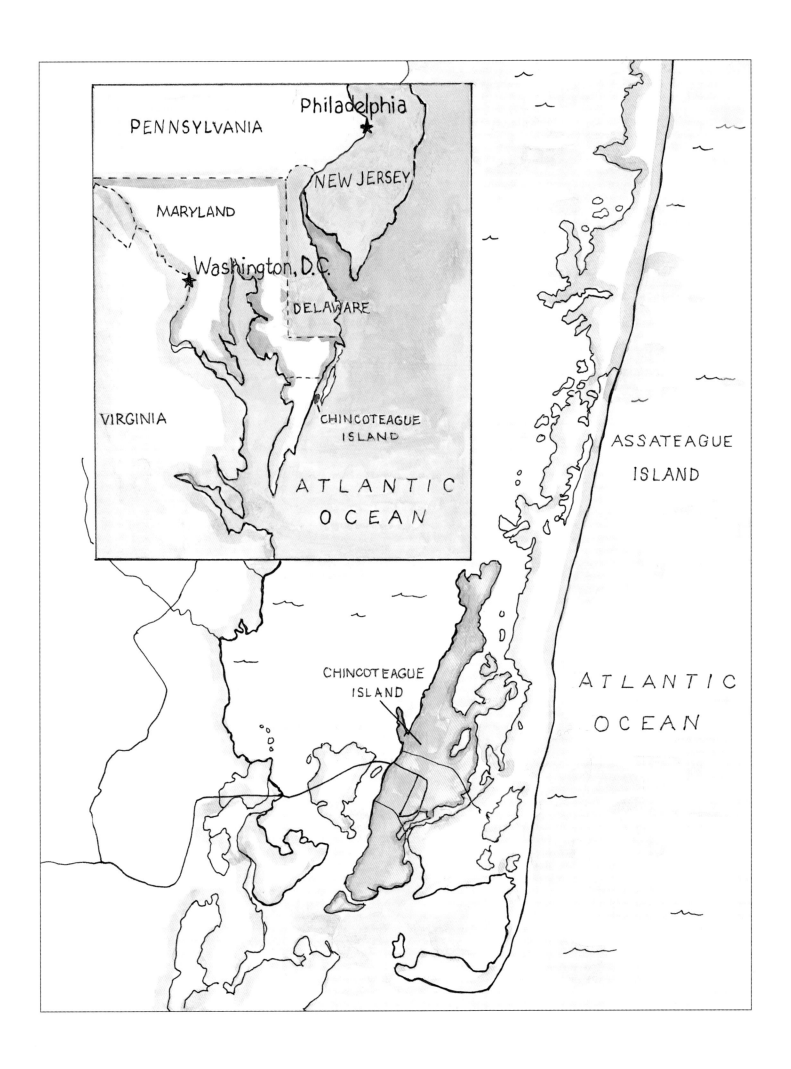

PENNSYLVANIA

Philadelphia

NEW JERSEY

MARYLAND

Washington, D.C.

DELAWARE

VIRGINIA

CHINCOTEAGUE
ISLAND

ATLANTIC
OCEAN

ASSATEAGUE
ISLAND

CHINCOTEAGUE
ISLAND

ATLANTIC

OCEAN

MARGUERITE HENRY

Dear Susan ———

Your letter gave me a most happy feeling.
THREE JOVIAL HUNTSMEN is my first autographed
book done by a long-time reader and fan of
Wesley Dennis. I wish he were here to
share in the joy, for I share your appreciation
of his horses, and the spirit beneath the hide and hair

Somehow, working on books hasn't been as
much fun without him. On his drawing
board he had a little hand written reminder:
"If it isn't fun, don't do it." And he never did.

"All the Pretty Horses" creates a dream mood that
waxes more and more exciting as dreams are
wont to do. Your horses in action are all any
dreamer could wish for. In repose, too. Mice are
very nice!

Congratulations! Do keep me informed of any change of
address.
                    Sincerely,
                    Marguerite Henry

This is a true story. Actually, it is several true stories.

Some years ago my sister, Judy, and I attended the auction of ponies at Pony Penning Day on Chincoteague Island, Virginia. We were touched when a foal bought at the auction was returned and then resold to a little girl with red hair. We watched as strangers in the audience passed singles, tens, and twenties to the amazed and grateful child, making her dream come true.

I was enchanted by this event, which seems to repeat itself every year. I have looked in local newspapers for stories about similar acts of generosity and have found at least one every summer. I was particularly impressed by the story of one young lady who had been the beneficiary of kindness from the people around her. After taking her pony home, she spent the next year working and saving her money. She returned to the auction the following summer with her savings, in order to help another child buy a pony.

That brought tears to my eyes.

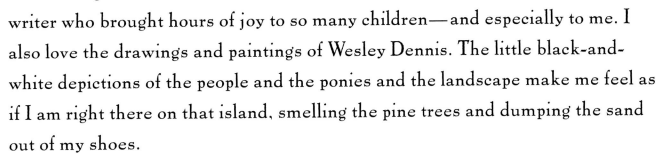

I fell in love with the story of the Chincoteague ponies when I was seven years old. That Christmas, my father brought home a signed copy of Marguerite Henry's *Misty of Chincoteague*. He had probably stood on line at Macy's for hours waiting for the author to sign his copy. From time to time I still run my fingers over her signature to connect with that extraordinary writer who brought hours of joy to so many children—and especially to me. I also love the drawings and paintings of Wesley Dennis. The little black-and-white depictions of the people and the ponies and the landscape make me feel as if I am right there on that island, smelling the pine trees and dumping the sand out of my shoes.

Years later, I sent copies of two of my books to Marguerite Henry to thank her for inspiring me. You can see her gracious response here.

Julie loved ponies.

Her room was filled with them.
She read *Misty of Chincoteague* over and over again.

On the dairy farm where she lived, there were cows and chickens, but no ponies.

Sometimes she would visit her friend Sharon's horse, Shanti.
She loved his soft muzzle and the way he breathed on her hand.
He was gentle and took her wherever she asked him to go.

But she longed for a pony of her own.

Julie knew that every July there was a pony auction on Chincoteague Island in Virginia. After months of trying, she finally convinced her parents that she could earn enough money to buy one of the famous ponies. Maybe there would be one that no one else wanted, or one that didn't cost too much.

Julie raked leaves, fed the chickens, and babysat her cousins. She cleared out the toolshed and put straw down for a soft bed. It was the perfect home for a new pony.

At last it was July. While Dad stayed home to take care of the farm, Julie and her mother drove to Chincoteague Island for Pony Penning Day.

As they crossed the bridge to Chincoteague, they could see nearby Assateague Island, where the ponies run free.

Julie knew the legend of the ponies. Many, many years ago, a Spanish galleon was said to have been shipwrecked off Assateague Island. It spilled its cargo of ponies into the sea. The ponies swam ashore and survived on the island.

The ponies learned to live on Assateague through all the seasons. They grew strong and beautiful, and new babies were born every year.

But soon there were too many ponies and not enough food for them all. So every summer, the fire department of Chincoteague Island holds a roundup of the pony herd on Assateague.

Fire department volunteers, known as "saltwater cowboys," swim some of the ponies across a narrow channel from Assateague to Chincoteague.

Then the cowboys carefully guide the ponies to the fairgrounds in town.

The evening before the auction, Julie and her mother went to the pens at the fairgrounds and looked at all the ponies. Julie felt as if her heart would burst, the ponies were all so beautiful.

A black-and-white filly came over and looked at Julie.

"If you were mine," whispered Julie, "I would call you Dream . . . Painted Dream."

The next morning Julie was too excited to eat. She and her mom headed straight for the auction.

Julie soon realized that she did not have enough money. She kept raising her hand to make a bid, but every time, the price climbed too high.

Julie's eyes filled with tears as one pony after another was sold. Even the black-and-white filly.

"Don't give up," said a woman sitting next to her. "Keep calling out your bid. Persistence pays off!" And she handed Julie a twenty-dollar bill.

"Thank you, but we really can't—" Julie's mother began; but then a little boy gave Julie a dollar.

"It looks like everyone wants you to have a pony of your own," her mother said, smiling.

"Thank you!" Julie exclaimed as more strangers passed her money.

Her heart leaped. Now she might have enough to buy her pony!

But it was too late. All the ponies had been sold.

As the last ponies were being taken out of the auction arena, a man shouted, "Wait! A pony has been returned. The barn where she was going won't take a foal."

"Don't leave, folks," the auctioneer said. "We have one more pony to sell."

It was the black-and-white pony, Painted Dream!

The auctioneer looked straight at Julie. Her heart pounded and her hand shot in the air. "Going once, going twice—sold to the little girl in the first row!"

"Well," said her mother, "what are you going to do now that you have your dream?"

"I have a lot of work to do," said Julie. "First I have to gentle my pony. Then I am going to do chores, save all my money, and come back next year."

"Isn't one pony enough?" her mother asked, laughing.

"No," said Julie. "I am going to give my money to another girl so that she can buy a pony of her own."

And that is just what she did.